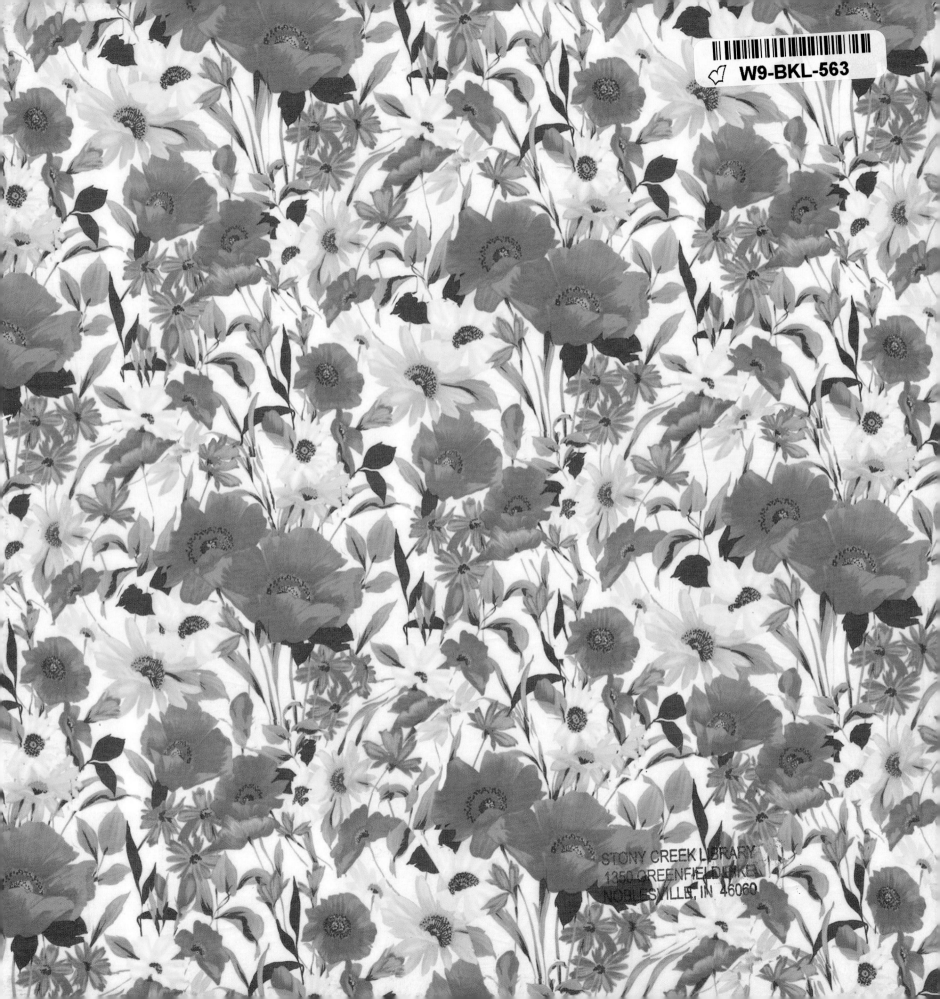

EPOSSUMONDAS PLAYS POSSUM

WRITTEN BY **Coleen Salley**

ILLUSTRATED BY **Janet Stevens**

HARCOURT CHILDREN'S BOOKS

Houghton Mifflin Harcourt

Boston   New York   2009

One summer morning as butterflies flitted between the zinnias, Epossumondas and his mama were sipping sweet tea and chitchatting about this and that.

"Look, Mama—that butterfly just flew right into the swamp all by itself," said Epossumondas. "Why do you always tell *me* not to go in the swamp by myself?"

"Land sakes, sugar pie, the swamp is scary and dangerous!" Mama said. "Paths go every which-a-way. You head down one path, then another, and first thing you know you're all turned around and lost. And you don't want to get lost in the swamp—

because something's in there just waiting for little possums like you!"

"What is it, Mama?"

"It's the loup-garou!"

"What's a loup-garou, Mama?"

"I'm not sure, honey, but I suppose it looks like the most awful thing you could imagine."

"What does the loup-garou sound like, Mama?"

"I don't know, sweetie, but some say it has the scariest snarl you ever heard. Others say it has the meanest hiss, and some say it has the loudest snort!"

"What does the loup-garou do, Mama?"

"Oh, that's the worst of all. If little possums don't mind their mamas, the loup-garou snatches them right up with its big ugly claws! So stay clear of the swamp, Epossumondas, and you'll be just fine. Now I'll go inside and fix our lunch."

Epossumondas went back to thinking about this and that. The loup-garou . . . the swamp . . . the butterflies . . . and when the prettiest butterfly he ever saw flew by, he started thinking about chasing it.

Now, those of you who've met
Epossumondas know that he's not a
naughty possum. But he *is* a forgetful
possum. And when he saw that butterfly,
he plumb forgot about the loup-garou.

Without a thought of what Mama had said, Epossumondas ran after that butterfly. You know where it went?

Right into the swamp.

And so did Epossumondas.

He went off this way—no butterfly.
He went off that way—no butterfly.
He ran down path after path, every
which-a-way—no butterfly.

Epossumondas stopped. "Which way do I go?" he wondered. "I'm lost!" He remembered Mama's warning now, but he was too deep into the swamp to find his way back. Then, near a clump of cypress trees, he heard . . . *Rrrrrrrr! Rrrrrrrr! Rrrrrrrr!*

"That's the scariest snarl I ever heard!" Epossumondas gasped. "It must be the loup-garou! What'll I do?" Then he flopped back, legs up, eyes shut, perfectly still—just like a good possum should.

Rrrrrrrr! Rrrrrrrr! Rrrrrrrr! The critter came closer and closer . . .

. . . and closer. *Rrrrrrrrr!* "Hey, this possum is dead!" it snarled.
"I don't eat no dead meat." And it padded off down the path.

Epossumondas opened his eyes. "Aw, that's no loup-garou—it's just a ferocious, terrifying ol' critter-eating swamp cat! So I'm not scared one little bit!"

But before he could run off, he heard . . .
Ssssss! Sssssss! Ssssssss!

"That's the meanest hiss I ever heard!"
Epossumondas gasped. "It must be the
loup-garou!" So he flopped back down,
legs up, eyes shut, perfectly still—just
like a good possum should.

Ssssss! Sssssss! Ssssssss! That slithering
thing came closer and closer . . .

. . . and closer. *Ssssssss.* "Thissss possum is dead," it
hissed. "I don't eat no dead meat." And it slithered away.

Epossumondas opened his eyes. "Aw, that's no loup-garou—it's just a terrible, slimy ol' possum-swallowing swamp snake! So I'm not scared one little bit!"

But before Epossumondas could run off, he heard . . . *Snort! Snort! Snort!*

"That's the loudest snort I ever heard!" Epossumondas gasped. "It must be the loup-garou!" So he flopped back down, legs up, eyes shut, perfectly still—just like a good possum should.

Snort! Snort! Snort! The creature stomped closer and closer . . .

. . . and closer. *Snort.* "Huh, this possum is dead!" it snorted.
"I don't eat no dead meat." And it stomped away.

Epossumondas opened his eyes. "Aw, that's no loup-garou—it's just a nasty, crusty ol' varmint-chomping swamp hog! So I'm not scared one little bit."

But before he could run off, an enormous, cold,
dark shadow moved over him. A shadow with wings.
A shadow with claws.

"Those big ugly claws will snatch me up, just like
Mama said!" Epossumondas gasped. "It must be the
loup-garou!" So he stayed down, legs up, eyes shut,
perfectly still—just like a good possum should.

He felt the shadow come closer and closer . . .

. . . and closer. And then those huge claws *did* take hold of Epossumondas and snatched him right up. Was he scared? Maybe—but he was also ticklish. Really ticklish. He started wiggling and jiggling and giggling. He just couldn't help it.

That shadow opened its claws and dropped Epossumondas like
a hot potato. "Why, this varmint ain't dead!" it squawked. "I never,
ever eat no *live* meat!" And it flapped away.

Epossumondas looked up. "Aw, that's no loup-garou—it's just a
creepy, smelly ol' bone-picking swamp buzzard! So I'm not scared one
little bit."

As Epossumondas lay there all worn out from playing dead, wondering how he would ever find his way home, he heard, "Honey, where are you? Epossumondas, you answer Mama!"

Epossumondas hollered, "Mama! Mama, I'm here!" In less than a minute he saw his mama running toward him. "Oh, Mama!" he cried. "I forgot what you said and I went in the swamp all by myself!"

Mama scooped him up. "Sugar, you need to listen to me! I was worried sick that the loup-garou had gotten you! You must've been scared to death."

"Oh, no, Mama, I didn't even see the loup-garou!" Epossumondas laughed. "All I saw was a ferocious, terrifying ol' critter-eating swamp cat—and then a terrible, slimy ol' possum-swallowing swamp snake—and then a nasty, crusty ol' varmint-chomping swamp hog—and then a creepy, smelly ol' bone-picking swamp buzzard that snatched me right up! So I wasn't scared one little bit."

"You saw *what?* Epossumondas, Epossumondas! You don't have the sense you were born with! You gotta run away from *those* fearsome critters, too!"

"But Mama, I do have the sense I was born with!" said Epossumondas. "I just played dead, like every good possum should!"

"Well, you sure are my clever little patootie," Mama told him. "Now, I think we've both had enough excitement for one day. Let's go find ourselves some of that sweet tea."

So Epossumondas and his mama headed
down the path toward home.

A Note from the Author

The *loup-garou*—an old French word for *werewolf*—has long been part of Louisiana lore. The legend of the loup-garou came to the Deep South with European settlers who continued to pass stories down to the next generations. Although the loup-garou is most often thought to be part wolf, part human, in the South it's also an elusive swamp creature with mysterious characteristics. What does it look like? What does it sound like? And is it real? No one really knows.

Any possum that encounters a threatening creature naturally uses the defense mechanism of playing dead (or "playing possum") in order to divert the danger—and surely any possum would use that skill against the loup-garou. Just like Epossumondas!

Text copyright © 2009 by The Estate of Coleen Salley   Illustrations copyright © 2009 by Janet Stevens
All rights reserved. Requests for permission to make copies of any part of the work should be submitted online at www.harcourt.com / contact or mailed to the following address: Permissions Department, Houghton Mifflin Harcourt Publishing Company, 6277 Sea Harbor Drive, Orlando, Florida 32887-6777.

Harcourt Children's Books is an imprint of Houghton Mifflin Harcourt Publishing Company.
www.hmhbooks.com

The illustrations in this book were done in mixed media on watercolor paper,
with selected effects created with the brushes of Obsidian Dawn.
The text type was set in Big Dog.   The display type was set in Couchlover.

Library of Congress Cataloging-in-Publication Data

Salley, Coleen.
Epossumondas plays possum / by Coleen Salley; illustrated by Janet Stevens.
p. cm.

Summary: Forgetting his mother's warnings, Epossumondas goes into the swamp alone and must pretend to be dead time and again as he hears frightening sounds and fears they are being made by the dreaded loup-garou.

ISBN 978-0-15-206420-4 [1. Opossums—Fiction. 2. Swamp animals—Fiction. 3. Fear—Fiction. 4. Swamps—Fiction. 5. Louisiana—Fiction.] I. Stevens, Janet, ill. II. Title.
PZ7.S15327Epk 2009
[E]—dc22   2009007976

Printed in Singapore   TWP 10 9 8 7 6 5 4 3 2 1

For my dearest friends, Ashley Bryan, Jean Craighead George,
Charlotte Zolotow, and Bill Morris. So much love and so many memories.

—C.S.

For my dear friend Coleen. I miss you.

—J.S.